Sweetest Kulu

by Celina Kalluk

Illustrated by Alexandria Neonakis

Sweetest Kulu,

on the day you were born, all of the Arctic Summer was there to greet you.

Smiling Sun shone so bright and stayed through the night,

giving you blankets and ribbons of warm light.

Melodies of Wind arrived,
sharing stories of how the weather forms, and telling you to always listen closely.
Wise Wind had learned your name, charming Kulu, and invited the world to meet you.

You had many wondrous and grand visitors!
They shared thoughts, feelings, and best wishes with you,
darling Kulu.

Adventurous Snow Bunting gifted you seeds from Arctic cotton,
and flowers for you to plant and grow with,
reminding you to always believe in yourself,
happy Kulu.

Arctic Hare, with rock willow and roots,
came to show you love so easily.
You became a best friend, baby Kulu, loving to give.

Fox, so thoughtful and swift,
came to tell you to get out of bed as soon as you wake,
and to help anyone who may need help along your way,
admired Kulu.

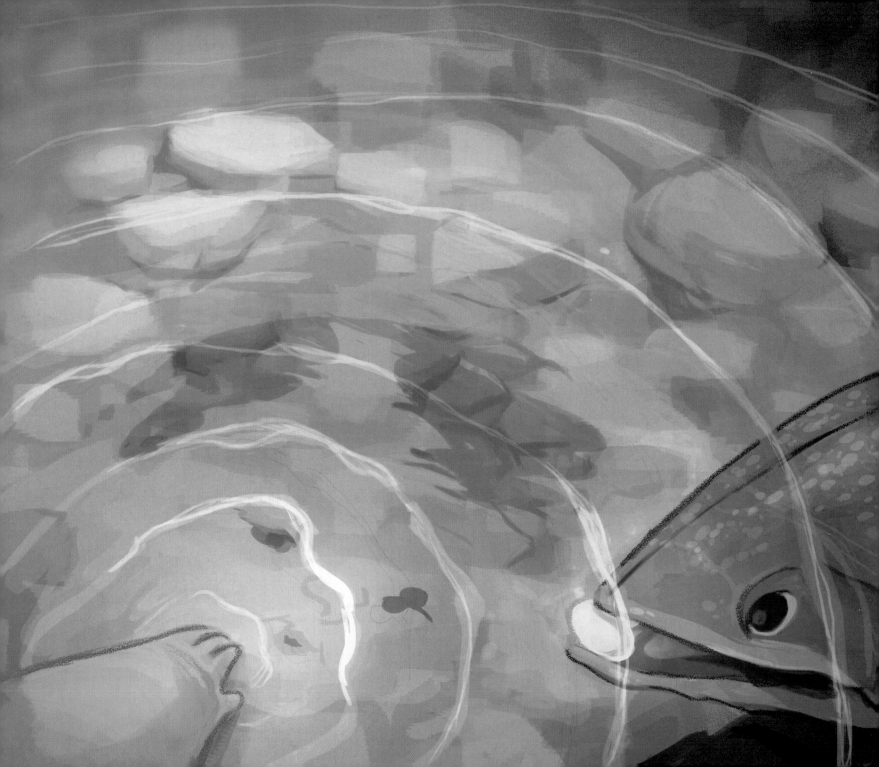

Thinking of you,
Arctic Char enjoyed reflections in waters so sea green,
and gave you tenderness, too, beautiful and handsome Kulu.

Seal, whose favourite colour is ice blue,

heard about Arctic Char's adoration of you.

Seal loves creativity, and surrounded you with colour, nicest Kulu.

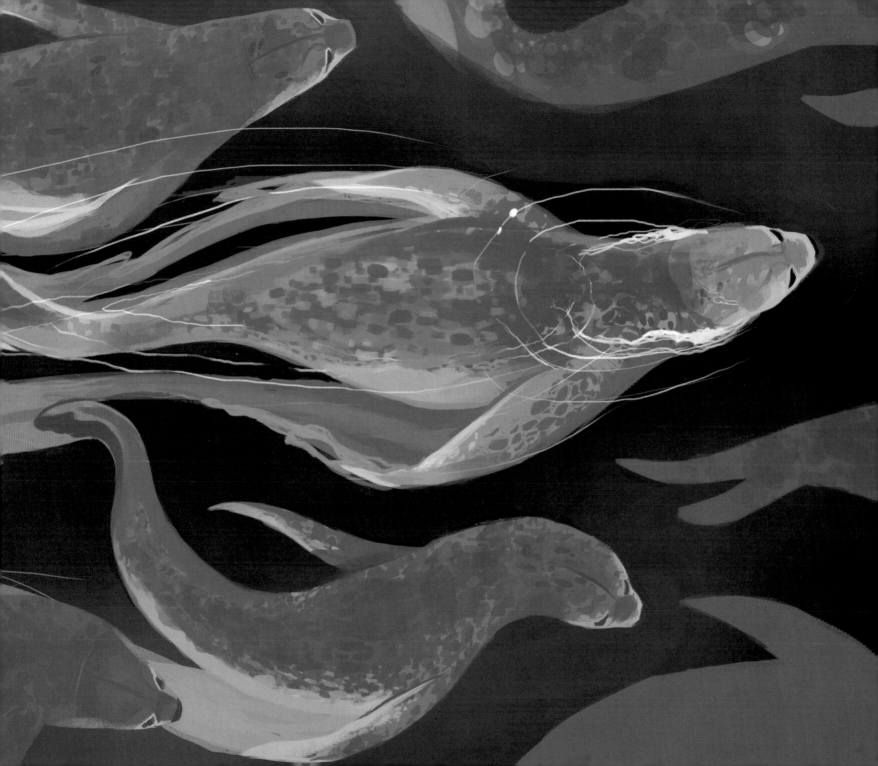

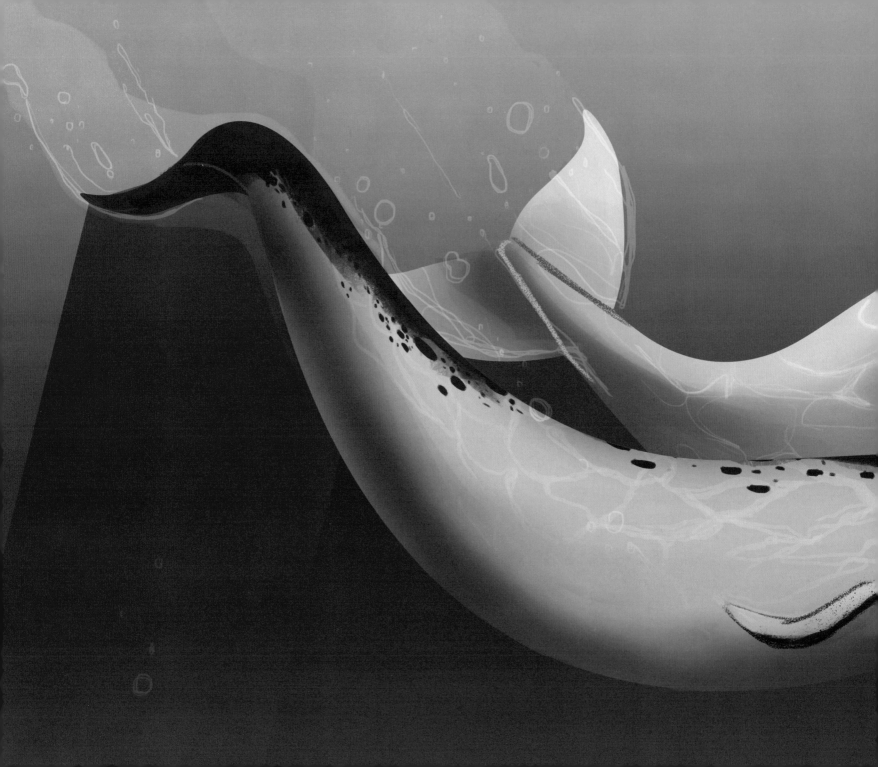

Narwhal and Beluga saw the natural gift to the world that you are.
They gave you spontaneity, little Kulu,
and the joyful feeling that comes with finishing well what you start.

Muskox shared heritage and empowerment with you,
magnificent Kulu,
showing you how to protect what you believe in.

Caribou chose patience for you, cutest Kulu.
He gave you the ability to look to the stars, so that you will always
know where you are and may gently lead the way.

Polar Bear, with powerful instinct,
taught you to always treat animals with respect and to never scold them.
Polar Bear made an offering of gentleness, making you a modest
and kind Kulu.

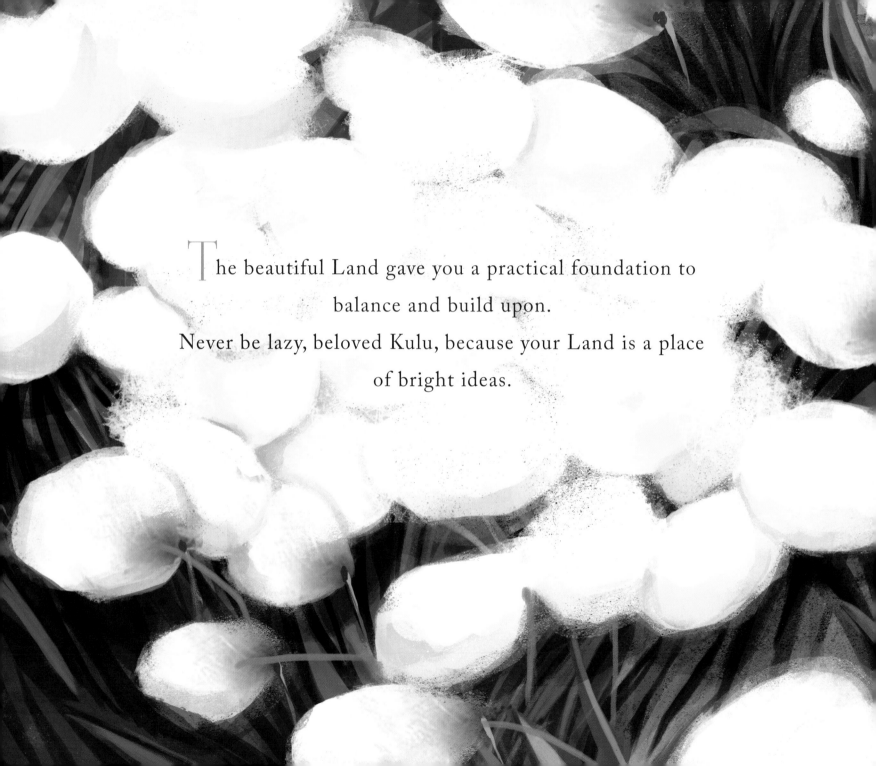

The beautiful Land gave you a practical foundation to
balance and build upon.
Never be lazy, beloved Kulu, because your Land is a place
of bright ideas.

Dream a little, Kulu, this world now sings a
most beautiful song of you.
Slumber in safety.
Tomorrow will wait patiently.
Be calm, Kulu, and celebrate,
because you are true love.

Celina Kalluk was born and raised in Resolute Bay, Nunavut, to Zipporah Kalluk and Leonard Thibodeau. Celina has two brothers and five sisters, one sister-niece, and many more beautiful nieces and nephews. She also has four daughters of her own, Jazlin, Aulaja, Saima, and Ramata. She dedicates this book to all the mothers and fathers of this earth and to our wonderful children. Celina is also a visual artist and has illustrated several book covers and other literacy materials. Currently, she is the Inuktitut Language Specialist and Cultural Arts teacher for grades seven through twelve at Qarmartalik School in Resolute Bay. *Sweetest Kulu* is her first book for children.

Alexandria Neonakis is an illustrator and designer from Dartmouth, Nova Scotia. She currently lives with her cat, "Kitty," in Santa Monica, California.

Published by Inhabit Media Inc.
www.inhabitmedia.com

Inhabit Media Inc. (Iqaluit), P.O. Box 11125, Iqaluit, Nunavut, X0A 1H0
(Toronto), 146A Orchard View Blvd., Toronto, Ontario, M4R 1C3

Design and layout copyright © 2014 Inhabit Media Inc.
Text copyright © 2014 Celina Kalluk
Illustrations by Alexandria Neonakis copyright © 2014 Inhabit Media Inc.

Editors: Neil Christopher and Kelly Ward
Art director: Danny Christopher

We acknowledge the financial support of the Government of Canada through the Department of Canadian Heritage Canada Book Fund.

We acknowledge the support of the Canada Council for the Arts for our publishing program.

ISBN: 978-1-927095-77-5

Printed in Canada

Library and Archives Canada Cataloguing in Publication

Kalluk, Celina, author
       Sweetest Kulu / by Celina Kalluk ; illustrated by
Alexandria Neonakis.

ISBN 978-1-927095-77-5 (bound)

       I. Neonakis, Alexandria, illustrator II. Title.

PS8621.A473S93 2014   jC811'.6   C2014-904985-4